Guardian Of The Heart

Mrigendra Bharti

Published by Sellbrochure Vymish Entertainment, 2024.

This is a work of fiction. Similarities to real people, places, or events are entirely coincidental.

GUARDIAN OF THE HEART

First edition. June 28, 2024.

Copyright © 2024 Mrigendra Bharti.

ISBN: 979-8224941049

Written by Mrigendra Bharti.

Table of Contents

Preface 1

Prologue 3

About Sellbrochure Vymish Entertainment 5

Introduction 8

Chapter 1: A Shrouded Silence 12

Chapter 2: Whispers of the Past 23

Chapter 3: The Whispering Walls 35

Chapter 4: Whispers on the Wind 46

Chapter 5: Echoes in the Stone 58

Conclusion 70

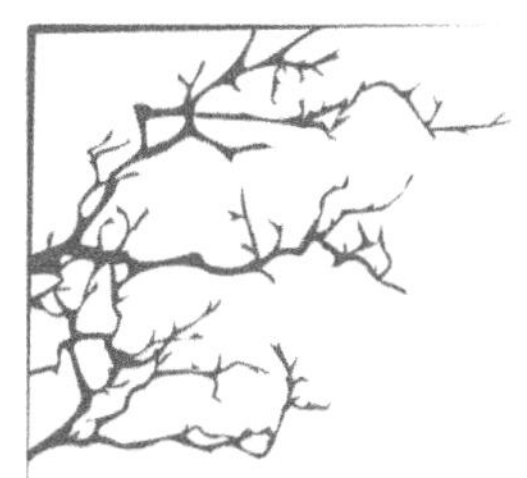

Preface

The whispers began as a faint murmur, carried on the wind that danced through the Whispering Walls, a vast network of caverns shrouded in legend and mystery. These whispers spoke of a hidden power, a slumbering giant nestled deep within the mountain's heart.

For generations, our village existed in a fragile peace, nestled beneath the watchful gaze of these ancient walls. We knew the stories, the warnings passed down from our ancestors. We knew of the Shadows, creatures of darkness that thirsted for the power said to reside within. But the whispers were just that – whispers, a distant echo in the vast tapestry of our existence.

Then came the day the whispers grew louder, a chilling melody that spoke of a prophecy unfolding. A prophecy that spoke of a chosen one, a young soul destined to face the darkness and protect the slumbering power from falling into the wrong hands.

This book is not just the chronicle of a perilous journey, a descent into the labyrinthine depths of the Whispering Walls. It is a testament to the courage that lies dormant within even the most innocent hearts. It is a story of responsibility, of the burden of power, and the unwavering belief that even the smallest spark of light can illuminate the darkest corners.

As you turn the pages, prepare to be transported to a world where ancient secrets whisper in the wind, where courage and wisdom are the only weapons against the encroaching shadows. Prepare to be captivated by the tale of Parvati and Shaurya, two young villagers thrust into a destiny far greater than they could have ever imagined.

This is their story, a story etched not just in the pages of this book, but in the very fabric of our village's history. Let it serve as a reminder that the echoes of hope can resonate far louder than the whispers of fear.

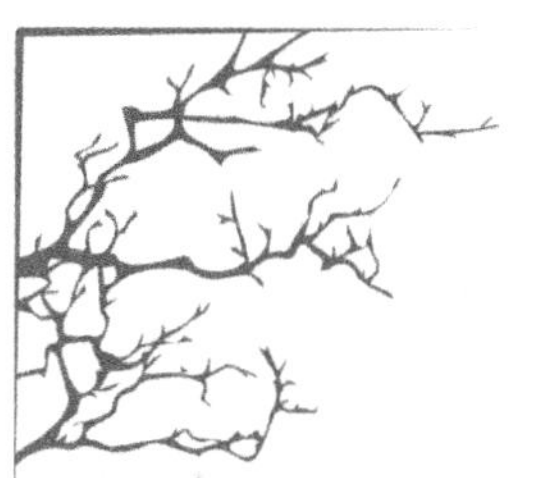

Prologue

The wind howled a mournful song through the jagged teeth of the Whispering Walls, a vast network of caverns that sliced through the mountain's heart. Legends, whispered down through generations, painted these caverns as a place of immense power, a slumbering giant waiting to be awakened. But for the villagers who lived nestled in the mountain's shadow, the Whispering Walls were more than a source of unsettling folklore; they were a tangible reminder of a fragile peace.

One evening, as the dying embers of the sun painted the sky in hues of orange and purple, an old woman named Anya sat by the flickering fire, her face etched with the wisdom of a life well-lived. Her wrinkled hands traced a symbol on the rough-hewn stone hearth, a symbol passed down through her bloodline – a symbol of guardianship.

A young girl, Parvati, Anya's granddaughter, sat mesmerized by the flickering firelight. Curiosity danced in her dark eyes. "Nana," she whispered, her voice barely audible over the wind's mournful cry, "tell me again about the stories. About the Shadows and the power that sleeps within the Walls."

Anya sighed, a deep rumble that echoed the wind's song. "These are stories for a time of peace, little one," she said, her voice raspy with age. "Stories to remind us of the darkness that lurks beyond the light of our village fire."

Parvati persisted, her voice filled with a youthful yearning for adventure. "But what if the darkness awakens? What if the whispers turn into screams?"

Anya's gaze hardened. "Then," she said, her voice gaining strength, "the guardians will awaken too. Chosen ones, marked by the symbol of our lineage, will face the shadows and protect the slumbering power, just as my ancestors did before me."

Parvati shivered, a thrill mingled with a flicker of fear dancing on her skin. The symbol on the hearth seemed to glow with a faint light, as if responding to Anya's words. A silence settled upon them, broken only by the relentless wind and the crackling fire. In that moment, under the watchful gaze of the Whispering Walls, a seed of destiny was sown, a seed that would soon blossom into a storm.

About Sellbrochure
Vymish
Entertainment

Sellbrochure Vymish Entertainment, recognized as India's largest book publishing company, has made significant strides in ensuring its extensive collection of books reaches audiences across the global market. This rapid expansion is a testament to the company's dedication to disseminating knowledge and literature far beyond national borders. Central to its success is its affiliation with InkWhirl Media Networks, a reputable entity in the media and publication industry known for its innovative and strategic approaches. Within this network, InkWhirl Publication LLC operates as a vital division, further enhancing the company's capabilities and reach in the international market.

The visionary behind this enterprise is Mrigendra Bharti, the founder of Sellbrochure Vymish Entertainment. His foresight and passion for the literary world have been instrumental in steering the company towards remarkable growth and recognition. Under his leadership, Sellbrochure Vymish Entertainment has not only expanded its catalog but also established a strong presence in both domestic and international markets. Mrigendra Bharti's commitment to excellence and innovation has been a driving force in the company's journey, ensuring that it stays ahead of industry trends and meets the evolving needs of readers worldwide.

Sellbrochure Vymish Entertainment operates under the robust support of its parental organization, Mrigendra Bharti Group InfoTech. This affiliation provides the necessary resources and strategic guidance, enabling the publishing company to undertake ambitious projects and explore new markets. Mrigendra Bharti Group InfoTech's extensive experience in technology and information services has been a valuable asset, allowing Sellbrochure Vymish Entertainment to integrate advanced digital solutions in its operations, thereby enhancing its distribution capabilities and reader engagement.

Through relentless efforts and a commitment to quality, Sellbrochure Vymish Entertainment continues to break barriers and expand the reach of Indian literature globally. The company's diverse portfolio includes a wide range of genres, catering to different age groups and interests, thereby fostering a rich and inclusive reading culture. As it continues to innovate and grow, Sellbrochure Vymish Entertainment remains dedicated to its mission of making literature accessible to all, contributing significantly to the global literary landscape.

Connect With Mrigendra,
Thank you very much for choosing this book.
You can also connect with me on Instagram,
https://www.instagram.com/i_mrigendrabharti.official
With Love,
Mrigendra Bharti

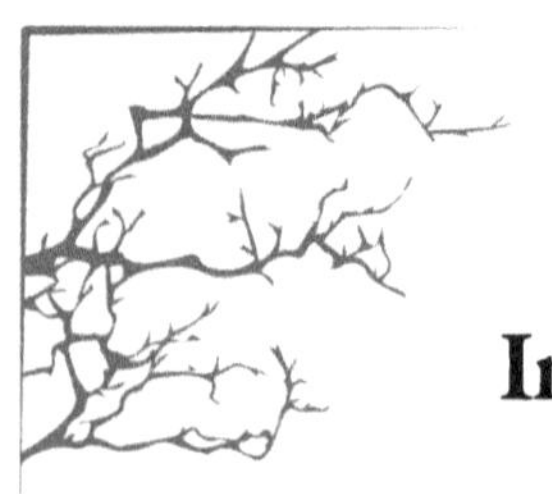

Introduction

The wind, a relentless nomad, forever danced through the jagged teeth of the Whispering Walls. These weren't mere cliffs; they were titans of stone, carved by time and shrouded in an aura of ancient mystery. Legends, passed down through generations in hushed tones around crackling fires, spoke of an intricate network of caverns within these walls, a labyrinthine heart pulsing with a hidden power.

The village, nestled like a sleepy child in the cradle of the valley below, knew these stories well. They were a constant murmur, a reminder of a fragile peace, a whisper against the symphony of crickets and chirping birds that filled their days. The whispers spoke of the Shadows, malignant entities that lurked within the walls, their very existence a threat to the slumbering power they so desperately coveted.

But for generations, these whispers remained a bedtime story, a warning passed down with a nudge and a wink, a cautionary tale more myth than reality. The villagers lived simple lives, content with the rhythm of the seasons and the familiar faces that surrounded them. The Whispering Walls were a constant presence, yet distant, their jagged profile a silhouette against the changing hues of the sky.

Then one day, the wind changed. It no longer carried the gentle song of the valley, but a mournful howl, a chilling melody that seemed to emanate from the very heart of the mountain itself. The whispers, once faint murmurs carried on the night breeze, grew louder, a chilling crescendo that spoke of a prophecy unfolding.

This prophecy, whispered on the wind for centuries, spoke of a chosen one, a young soul destined to face the darkness and protect the slumbering power from falling into the wrong hands. It was a time of unease, a subtle shift in the air that prickled the skin and sparked a disquietude in the hearts of the villagers. The whispers, now an unsettling reality, filled the silence between conversations and lingered in the shadows at dusk.

Enter Parvati, a young girl with eyes that held the wisdom of a moonlit sky and a spirit as bright as the midday sun. Curiosity danced in her gaze as she sat mesmerized by the flickering firelight, listening to her grandmother, Anya, recount the tales of the past. Anya, a woman deeply etched with the wisdom of a life well-lived, traced a symbol on the rough stone hearth – a symbol passed down through their lineage, a symbol of guardianship.

"Nana," Parvati whispered, her voice barely audible over the growing wind, "tell me again about the stories. About the Shadows and the power that sleeps within the Walls."

Anya sighed, a deep rumble that resonated in the hearth's warmth. "These are stories for a time of peace, little one," she said, her voice raspy with age, "stories to remind us of the darkness that lurks beyond the light of our village fire."

Parvati persisted, her voice filled with a youthful yearning for adventure. "But what if the darkness awakens? What if the whispers turn into screams?"

Anya's gaze hardened, the firelight reflected in her eyes with an intensity that startled Parvati.

"Then," she said, her voice gaining strength, "the guardians will awaken too. Chosen ones, marked by the symbol of our lineage, will face the shadows and protect the slumbering power, just as my ancestors did before me."

Parvati shivered, a thrill mingled with a flicker of fear dancing on her skin. The symbol on the hearth seemed to glow with a faint light, as if responding to Anya's words. A silence settled upon them, broken only by the relentless wind and the crackling fire. In that moment, under the watchful gaze of the Whispering Walls, a seed of destiny was sown, a seed that would soon blossom into a storm.

Years passed, and Parvati grew into a young woman, her childhood curiosity tempered with the wisdom of her lineage. The whispers remained, a constant reminder of the prophecy and the potential threat that loomed. Yet, life in the village continued at its unhurried pace.

Parvati learned the art of weaving, her nimble fingers crafting intricate patterns on the loom, each thread carrying the story of her ancestors. Her life was a tapestry woven with the laughter of friends, the warmth of family, and the quiet contentment of a life lived in harmony with nature.

One day, the wind returned, carrying with it not just a chilling melody but a tangible shift in the air, a thickening of the atmosphere that tasted of fear. The whispers transformed into screams, echoing through the village with a desperate urgency. The villagers huddled together, their faces etched with terror. The Shadows, once figments of forgotten stories, were no longer whispers in the dark; they were a terrifying reality clawing at the edges of their world.

Parvati, her heart pounding in her chest, felt the symbol on her hand throb with a strange heat.

Chapter 1: A Shrouded Silence

Nestled amidst the emerald embrace of Haryana's sprawling plains, lay the village of Suhana. A tapestry of tranquility woven with the golden threads of sunrises and the silver shimmer of moonlit nights, Suhana was a haven of serenity. The gentle murmur of the Saraswati River flowed like a lullaby, its lifeblood nourishing the fertile fields that stretched outwards from the village. Here, life moved at a leisurely pace, dictated by the rhythm of the seasons and the timeless cycle of nature. The villagers, a community bound by kinship and tradition, toiled in their fields, raised their cattle with gentle care, and gathered under the banyan tree in the village square each evening to share stories spun under the benevolent gaze of a star-studded sky.

Among these villagers lived two children, as different as night and day, yet bound by an invisible thread of friendship. Shaurya, a ten-year-old whirlwind of energy, was a constant source of mischief. His unruly mop of black hair defied all attempts at taming, and his eyes sparkled with an impish glint that perpetually hinted at his next prank. Parvati, on the other hand, was a nine-year-old embodiment of quiet wisdom. Unlike Shaurya's boisterous energy, she possessed a calmness that belied her age. Yet, a spark of curiosity flickered within her dark eyes, a silent observer of the world around her.

On the outskirts of Suhana, like a solitary sentinel guarding the village, stood a colossal mansion. Unlike the modest mud-brick houses that lined the village streets, the mansion was a stark contrast, a relic of a bygone era. Its imposing structure, shrouded in an air of mystery, seemed to whisper tales of a forgotten past. Towering walls, etched with the passage of time, encircled the property. A wrought iron gate, rusted by neglect, creaked ominously on its hinges, forever barring entry. The windows, like vacant eyes staring sightlessly outwards, were boarded shut, their emptiness adding to the mansion's brooding presence.

Legends swirled around the mansion, whispered on the wind like secrets best left untold. The elders spoke of a time when the mansion was a vibrant residence, home to a wealthy landowner and his family. But whispers turned to hushed tones as they recounted a tragedy, an unknown event that had plunged the mansion into darkness years ago. Since then, the mansion had stood like a mausoleum, a monument to a life abruptly extinguished.

The villagers steered clear of the mansion, its unsettling aura a constant reminder of the misfortune that had befallen its former inhabitants. Fear, a potent storyteller, had woven elaborate tales around the deserted structure. Some spoke of restless spirits that roamed the mansion's halls at night, their mournful cries echoing through the empty corridors. Others believed a dark sorcerer resided within, practicing forbidden magic that twisted the very fabric of reality. These tales, embellished with each retelling, sent shivers down the spines of even the bravest villagers.

Shaurya and Parvati, however, were far from being afraid. In fact, the mansion held a peculiar fascination for them. The forbidden whispers, the chilling tales – they all fueled their insatiable curiosity. Unlike the fearful villagers who avoided the mansion at all costs, Shaurya and Parvati found themselves drawn to its enigmatic presence. Evenings spent with other children were often filled with fantastical stories woven around the mansion, each vying to outdo the other with the most outlandish tale. But these were mere childish fancies, shared under the watchful gaze of adults, a safe distance away from the object of their fascination.

One sweltering summer evening, the oppressive heat hung heavy in the air. The relentless sun beat down mercilessly, and the only respite came from the shade of the sprawling mango orchard that bordered the village. Shaurya, Parvati, and a few of their friends found themselves engaged in a game of hide-and-seek amidst the orchard's labyrinthine embrace. Laughter echoed through the trees as they chased each other, their playful energy a stark contrast to the oppressive silence that enveloped the mansion on the other side of the orchard wall.

As the day began its descent, casting long shadows across the orchard floor, Parvati, designated as the seeker, embarked on her quest. She called out for her friends, her voice tinged with mock seriousness. One by one, she emerged triumphant, her friends skillfully hidden amongst the verdant foliage. Finally, only Shaurya remained unfound.

Parvati searched high and low, her initial amusement slowly morphing into concern. She called out his name repeatedly, but there was no response. Just as she was about to abandon the search and alert the others, a muffled giggle reached her ears.

It seemed to be coming from the far end of the orchard, near the towering wall that separated the orchard from the mansion grounds.

Curiosity overriding her apprehension, Parvati crept towards the source of the sound. The gnarled branches of the mango trees clawed at her clothes, and the thick undergrowth snagged at her bare feet. As she neared the wall, the giggling grew louder, punctuated by hushed whispers.

Peeking through a gap in the foliage, Parvati spotted Shaurya crouched behind a large, weathered boulder, his face contorted in a mischievous grin. Relief washed over her, momentarily eclipsing the flicker of annoyance at his deliberate attempt to prolong the game.

"There you are!" she exclaimed, emerging from her hiding place. "I thought I'd lost you."

Shaurya's grin faltered for a split second. He brushed a stray strand of hair from his eyes and looked towards the mansion with a feigned nonchalance.

"Lost me? Nah," he said, his voice betraying a hint of nervousness. "Just found a pretty cool hiding spot, that's all."

Parvati wasn't convinced. She knew Shaurya, and the way he was fidgeting and darting nervous glances towards the mansion told a different story.

"What is it?" she pressed, her voice a low murmur.

Shaurya hesitated, then leaned closer to her, his voice barely a whisper.

"I think I saw something," he confessed, his eyes wide with a mixture of excitement and fear.

Parvati's brow furrowed. "Saw what?"

"There was a light," Shaurya explained, his voice hushed. "Inside the mansion. A weird, blue light coming from one of the windows."

Parvati's breath hitched. The stories about the mansion, the whispers of ghosts and dark magic, suddenly felt more real than ever. A shiver ran down her spine despite the oppressive heat.

"A light?" she echoed, her voice barely above a whisper.

Shaurya nodded vigorously. "Yeah, it was flickering on and off. Like a... like a ghost light."

The mention of a ghost light sent a jolt of fear through Parvati. Yet, a spark of curiosity flickered within her, battling against the rising tide of apprehension.

They stood in silence for a moment, the weight of the forbidden mansion pressing down on them. The playful mood of the afternoon had vanished, replaced by a sense of unease. Finally, Parvati broke the silence.

"Maybe it's just the moonlight reflecting off something," she offered, her voice lacking conviction even to her own ears.

Shaurya shook his head stubbornly. "No, it wasn't like moonlight. It was different. It pulsed, you know, like a heartbeat."

The image of a pulsating blue light emanating from the darkness of the mansion sent shivers down Parvati's spine. The stories, once dismissed as mere fables, now seemed to hold a grain of truth.

A tense silence descended upon them, broken only by the chirping of crickets and the distant croaking of frogs. Shaurya and Parvati exchanged glances, a silent question hanging in the air between them. What were they going to do?

Suddenly, a new sound pierced the quiet – a low creaking noise, like an old hinge groaning in protest. It seemed to be coming from the direction of the mansion gate.

Shaurya and Parvati's hearts pounded in their chests. Their playful afternoon adventure had taken an unexpected and unsettling turn. Fear, cold and sharp, clawed at their insides. They looked at each other, a silent understanding passing between them. It was time to leave.

Without a word, they turned and began to retreat, their movements cautious and quiet. They weaved their way through the undergrowth, their eyes darting nervously towards the source of the creaking sound. As they reached the edge of the orchard, they paused for a moment, stealing a final glance towards the imposing silhouette of the mansion. The blue light was gone, the windows once again dark and vacant.

With a shared breath of relief, they quickened their pace, their laughter long forgotten. The playful game of hide-and-seek had morphed into a chilling encounter that left them shaken and unsure. The mansion, shrouded in an even deeper mystery, now held a terrifying allure for them. The question of the blue light, and the creaking sound from the gate, gnawed at their minds, a seed of fear and curiosity planted deep within them.

The walk back to the village was shrouded in an unsettling silence. Gone were the carefree giggles that had filled the afternoon air. Shaurya and Parvati walked shoulder to shoulder, their eyes fixed on the dusty path ahead. The playful banter that usually marked their adventures had evaporated, replaced by a heavy weight of unease.

Shaurya, usually the embodiment of boundless energy, seemed subdued. The encounter with the mysterious blue light and the ominous creaking noise had cast a shadow over his usual bravado. He stole glances at Parvati, seeking reassurance in her presence.

Parvati, ever the voice of reason, tried to rationalize what they had witnessed. "Maybe it was just an animal," she offered, her voice unconvincing even to herself.

Shaurya shook his head, his brow furrowed in thought. "But what about the light? It couldn't have been an animal that made a light like that, could it?"

Parvati couldn't offer a counterargument. The image of the pulsating blue light flickered in her mind, defying any logical explanation.

As they neared the village square, the familiar sights and sounds offered a sense of comfort. The flickering flames of oil lamps cast a warm glow, and the rhythmic clanging of the blacksmith's hammer provided a comforting backdrop. Villagers bustled about, their voices a soothing murmur.

Reaching the edge of the square, Shaurya and Parvati stopped, their gazes drawn towards a group of elders huddled beneath the sprawling banyan tree. The elders, their faces etched with the passage of time, were engaged in a heated discussion. Curiosity tugged at Parvati, momentarily pushing the unsettling events of the afternoon to the back of her mind.

"What do you think they're talking about?" she whispered to Shaurya.

Shaurya shrugged, his usual mischievous glint replaced by a flicker of worry. "Maybe something about the harvest or the upcoming festival."

Parvati wasn't convinced. The urgency in the elders' voices and the furrowed brows suggested a more pressing matter. But before they could investigate further, a call from Shaurya's mother shattered the tentative peace.

"Shaurya! There you are! Where have you been?" His mother's voice, laced with worry, cut through the evening air.

Shaurya mumbled an apology, relief washing over him at the sight of his familiar surroundings. His mother, her gaze lingering on his muddied clothes and scratched knees, ushered him home with a stern look.

Parvati watched them go, a pang of loneliness replacing the earlier fear. As Shaurya disappeared into the distance, she turned towards her own home, the weight of the afternoon's events settling heavily on her shoulders.

The image of the deserted mansion loomed large in her mind. The blue light, the creaking gate – these were not figments of their imagination. They had stumbled upon something unsettling, something that defied explanation.

Later that night, as Parvati lay nestled in her cot, the events of the day replayed in her mind. Sleep evaded her, replaced by a churning mix of fear and curiosity. The forbidden mansion, once a source of childish fascination, now held a terrifying allure.

She tossed and turned, the silence of the night broken only by the chirping of crickets. Finally, she reached a decision. She couldn't keep what they had witnessed a secret. She needed to confide in someone, someone who might have an explanation for the strange occurrences at the mansion.

With a newfound determination, Parvati resolved to speak to her grandmother, a woman known for her wisdom and knowledge of village lore. Perhaps her grandmother held the key to unraveling the mystery of the blue light and the secrets hidden within the walls of the deserted mansion.

The morning sun cast a golden glow on Suhana, washing away the unsettling memories of the previous evening. However, for Parvati, the events at the mansion lingered in her mind. The image of the blue light flickered behind her eyelids as she finished her breakfast, a stark contrast to the cheerful chatter around the table.

Unable to shake off the weight of the secret, Parvati made a plan. After breakfast, she would seek out her grandmother, Nani Amma, a woman known for her gentle wisdom and a deep well of knowledge about the village's history and folklore. Perhaps Nani Amma would have an explanation for the strange blue light and the unsettling creaking sound from the mansion gate.

With a stolen glance at her mother, busy with household chores, Parvati slipped out of the house. She weaved through the village streets, the familiar sights and sounds offering a comforting sense of normalcy. Reaching Nani Amma's small cottage, nestled amidst a profusion of vibrant flowers, Parvati took a deep breath and knocked softly on the weathered wooden door.

The rhythmic clatter of knitting needles stopped abruptly, followed by a gentle "Aao, beta" (Come in, child) from inside. Parvati pushed open the door, a wave of warmth and the comforting scent of spices enveloping her.

Nani Amma sat in a cozy armchair, her silver hair pulled back in a neat bun. Her wrinkled face, etched with the passage of time, bore the mark of a life lived fully. Her eyes, however, still held a youthful spark, twinkling with kindness and warmth.

Parvati hesitantly stepped inside, closing the door softly behind her. Nani Amma looked up, a smile gracing her lips.

"Parvati! It's good to see you," she said, her voice a soothing melody. "Come, sit here with me."

Parvati shuffled towards a stool opposite Nani Amma, her gaze flickering to the basket of colorful yarn and half-knitted shawl resting on her lap. Taking a deep breath, she blurted out, "Nani Amma, I need to tell you something."

Nani Amma placed her knitting down, her full attention focused on her granddaughter. "What is it, beta? Don't hesitate to speak your mind."

Parvati poured out her story, describing their encounter with the blue light and the unsettling creaking noise. She recounted the whispers and tales surrounding the mansion, her voice tinged with a mix of fear and fascination.

Nani Amma listened patiently, her eyes filled with a knowing glint. Once Parvati finished, a heavy silence settled in the room. Finally, Nani Amma spoke, her voice soft but firm.

"The stories about the mansion," she began, "have been around for many years. Some say it's haunted by the spirits of those who met a tragic end there. Others believe a dark sorcerer dwells within its walls."

Parvati's heart pounded in her chest. Nani Amma's words confirmed their suspicions, adding a layer of fear to the unsettling events.

"But Nani Amma," Parvati stammered, "what about the blue light? And the sound at the gate?"

Nani Amma didn't offer a definitive answer. Instead, she said, "The past is full of secrets, beta. Sometimes, things we don't understand exist beyond our comprehension."

Parvati was disappointed. She had yearned for a clear explanation, but Nani Amma's words resonated with a different kind of truth. The mansion, shrouded in an aura of mystery, held something powerful, something that defied easy explanation.

Sensing Parvati's dejection, Nani Amma patted her hand gently. "However," she continued, a spark of determination glinting in her eyes, "there might be someone who can shed more light on this. Have you heard of Panditji, the learned priest from the neighboring village?"

A flicker of hope ignited in Parvati's eyes.

Panditji, known for his wisdom and knowledge of ancient texts, might be the key to unraveling the mystery.

"No, Nani Amma," Parvati replied, her voice gaining strength. "But I can ask around."

Nani Amma smiled. "Good," she said.

"Sometimes, the most unexpected avenues lead to the answers we seek. But remember, beta, curiosity is a good thing, but recklessness is not. Be careful around the mansion, and don't do anything you're not comfortable with."

Parvati nodded, a newfound sense of purpose replacing her fear. Nani Amma's words served as a cautionary tale, yet fueled her determination to learn more. She couldn't ignore what they had witnessed. The blue light, the creaking gate – these were signs of something hidden within the walls of the mansion, a secret waiting to

Chapter 2: Whispers of the Past

The oppressive heat of summer finally surrendered to the gentle embrace of monsoon. The parched earth drank in the life-giving rain, and a vibrant tapestry of green unfolded across the plains surrounding Suhana. Yet, for Parvati, a storm of a different kind brewed within. The encounter with the blue light at the deserted mansion remained etched in her memory, a constant reminder of the secrets it held.

Nani Amma's words resonated within her. Curiosity, the spark that ignited most of her adventures, was now entangled with a sense of trepidation. The mansion, once a source of childish fascination, now appeared menacing, shrouded in an aura of mystery that both terrified and intrigued her.

Days turned into weeks, and the memory of the blue light began to fade, replaced by the daily routines of village life. The monsoon season painted the landscape with a vibrant green, and the villagers, their spirits lifted by the promise of a bountiful harvest, bustled with renewed energy.

Yet, for Parvati, a gnawing unease lingered.

One evening, as twilight painted the sky in hues of orange and purple, Parvati found herself drawn to the village square, a place where gossip and news often intertwined. A group of elders were huddled beneath the sprawling banyan tree, their weathered faces illuminated by the flickering flames of oil lamps. Parvati, ever the curious soul, edged closer, hoping to catch snippets of their conversation.

"Did you hear?" one of the elders, a wiry man with a thick salt-and-pepper beard, spoke, his voice hushed. "About Panditji's visit?"

A collective murmur rippled through the group. Panditji, the learned priest from the neighboring village, was a figure of respect and a repository of ancient knowledge. His visits, though infrequent, were always marked by a buzz of curiosity and anticipation.

"Yes," another elder, a woman with a kind face etched with wrinkles, chimed in. "He arrives tomorrow, seeking a rare medicinal herb said to grow only on the outskirts of our village."

Parvati's heart skipped a beat. Panditji, the answer Nani Amma had hinted at, was coming to Suhana. This was her chance, a chance to unlock the secrets of the blue light and the deserted mansion.

Unable to contain her excitement, Parvati blurted out, "Panditji? Can I meet him?"

The elders, startled by her sudden intrusion, turned their gaze towards her. A flicker of amusement danced in their eyes.

"Ah, Parvati," the wiry elder chuckled, "always curious, aren't you?"

Parvati, her cheeks flushed with embarrassment, mumbled an apology. However, she couldn't help but voice the question that burned within her.

"Can I ask him about... the mansion?" she stammered, her voice barely above a whisper.

The elders exchanged a knowing glance. The mansion and its unsettling aura were a constant undercurrent in village life. A shadow of concern crossed their faces.

The woman with the kind face placed a calloused hand on Parvati's shoulder. "The mansion," she said gently, "holds secrets best left undisturbed, child. But if you must ask Panditji, remember to do so with respect and caution."

Parvati nodded solemnly, a mix of apprehension and determination swirling within her. Sleep that night offered little solace. Visions of the desolate mansion and the pulsating blue light danced behind her closed eyelids. However, the prospect of meeting Panditji, a beacon of knowledge in the midst of the unknown, fueled her resolve.

The next day dawned bright and clear, the air washed clean by the recent rains. As the sun climbed higher in the sky, casting its warm rays upon the village, anticipation grew within Parvati. She spent the morning helping her mother with chores, her mind preoccupied with her plan. Finally, as midday approached, a ripple of excitement swept through the village. Panditji had arrived.

Panditji, a man of average height and build, exuded an aura of serenity. His eyes, deep and penetrating, seemed to hold the wisdom of ages. His saffron-colored robes and the sandalwood tilak on his forehead further accentuated his air of piety. The villagers, their faces etched with respect, greeted him warmly.

Parvati, her heart pounding in her chest, stood at a distance, observing. She waited patiently for an opportunity to approach him. Finally, as the elders engaged Panditji in conversation about the medicinal herb, Parvati saw her chance.

Taking a deep breath, she mustered her courage and approached him. Panditji, his gaze kind and gentle, turned towards her.

"Namaste, Panditji," Parvati stammered, her voice barely a whisper.

"Namaste, beta," Panditji replied, his voice a soothing balm. "What brings you here?"

Parvati hesitated, a knot of nervousness tightening in her stomach. Should she reveal everything about the encounter with the blue light and the unsettling sounds from the mansion? Or should she approach it cautiously, testing the waters first?

Gathering her courage, she decided on a measured approach. "Panditji," she began, "my Nani Amma told me about you, about your vast knowledge of ancient stories and legends."

Panditji smiled thoughtfully, his weathered face crinkling at the corners. "Your Nani Amma is a wise woman, child. And yes, I do possess some knowledge of the past."

Parvati took another deep breath. "There's a place near our village," she continued, her voice gaining confidence. "An old mansion that has been abandoned for many years."

A flicker of recognition crossed Panditji's eyes. He leaned forward slightly, his gaze fixed on Parvati. "The abandoned mansion," he confirmed. "Yes, I have heard whispers about it."

Parvati's heart pounded with excitement. Panditji knew about the mansion! Perhaps he could shed light on the mystery surrounding it.

"Do you know why it's abandoned?" she asked, her voice hardly above a whisper.

Panditji's brow furrowed thoughtfully. "The stories surrounding the mansion are shrouded in time, child. Some say it was once the residence of a wealthy landowner who suffered a tragic loss. Others believe it was cursed, tainted by dark magic."

Parvati shivered, a cold gust of fear washing over her despite the warmth of the afternoon sun. "Cursed?" she stammered.

Panditji placed a comforting hand on her shoulder. "These are just stories, beta," he said gently. "But sometimes, even stories hold a grain of truth."

Parvati felt a surge of curiosity battle with the rising tide of fear. "Is there anything else you know about the mansion, Panditji?" she pressed, her voice barely audible.

Panditji closed his eyes for a moment, seemingly lost in thought. "There might be an old text," he murmured, more to himself than to Parvati. "A chronicle that recounts the history of this region. It might hold some clues about the mansion."

Parvati's eyes widened. An old text? This was more than she had dared to hope for. "Where is this text, Panditji?" she asked eagerly.

Panditji opened his eyes, a hint of a smile playing on his lips. "The knowledge you seek lies within the walls of my own monastery, child. Far from Suhana."

Disappointment washed over Parvati. The thought of traveling to the monastery, a place she had never been, seemed daunting. "But... how will I get there?" she stammered.

Panditji's smile widened. "Perhaps," he said, a twinkle in his eyes, "curiosity might pave the way for an adventure."

Parvati's spirits lifted. An adventure! The notion of leaving Suhana, venturing into the unknown, ignited a spark of excitement within her. However, a nagging sense of responsibility lingered.

"But what about the blue light, Panditji?" she asked, her voice regaining its urgency. "The one I saw with Shaurya, coming from the mansion windows."

Panditji's smile vanished, replaced by a solemn expression. "The blue light," he said, his voice low and serious. "That's a different matter altogether. It could be something more... ominous."

Parvati's excitement waned, replaced by a growing apprehension. Panditji's words sent shivers down her spine. What was this "ominous" thing he hinted at? Could it be connected to the stories of curses and dark magic?

Sensing her fear, Panditji placed a reassuring hand on her shoulder. "Don't be afraid, child," he said gently. "But be cautious. The secrets of the mansion, especially those related to the blue light, should not be tampered with lightly."

Parvati pondered his words, the weight of his warning settling upon her. The prospect of a journey to the monastery, coupled with the unsettling truth about the blue light, presented a difficult choice. Curiosity burned bright within her, yet the fear of the unknown gnawed at her.

As Panditji continued his conversation with the elders, Parvati stood at a distance, a storm of emotions brewing within her. The mystery of the abandoned mansion had taken a new turn, a potentially dangerous one. She had to decide - would she pursue the truth, even if it meant venturing into the unknown?

Days turned into weeks after Panditji's visit. The memory of his words, both the promise of adventure and the chilling warning about the blue light, echoed in Parvati's mind. The once forgotten whispers about the mansion resurfaced, swirling around her like a malevolent fog.

Shaurya, her usual companion in mischief, had become engrossed in preparing for the upcoming harvest festival. His boundless energy and playful spirit offered a welcome respite from Parvati's internal turmoil. Yet, a part of her yearned to confide in him, to share the burden of the secret they stumbled upon.

One moonlit night, unable to contain her anxieties any longer, Parvati slipped out of her bed and made her way towards Shaurya's room. The gentle glow of a diya (oil lamp) emanated from beneath his door, casting long shadows across the courtyard floor. Taking a deep breath, she pushed open the creaky wooden door.

Shaurya lay nestled in his cot, fast asleep. The moonlight bathed his face in an ethereal glow, momentarily banishing the mischievous glint from his eyes. Parvati stood by his bedside, her heart pounding a frantic rhythm against her ribs.

Hesitantly, she reached out and gently placed a hand on his shoulder. Shaurya stirred, his eyelids fluttering open sleepily. He blinked a few times, focusing on Parvati's worried expression.

"Parvati?" he mumbled, his voice thick with sleep. "What's wrong?"

Parvati sat down on the edge of his cot, biting her lip in apprehension. "Shaurya," she began, her voice barely a whisper, "I need to tell you something."

She poured out the events of the past few weeks, recounting Panditji's visit, his knowledge of the mansion, and his ominous warning about the blue light. Shaurya listened intently, his sleepiness replaced by a growing curiosity and a hint of fear.

"A cursed mansion and a blue light?" he muttered, his eyes wide with wonder. "That sounds like something out of Nani Amma's bedtime stories.

Parvati shook her head. "This is different, Shaurya. Panditji said the blue light could be something dangerous.

Shaurya's face paled slightly. The playful glint that usually resided in his eyes had been replaced by a flicker of apprehension.

"So, what are you going to do?" he asked, his voice barely above a whisper.

Parvati looked down at her hands, a knot of indecision tightening in her stomach. "Panditji mentioned an old text," she said, "kept in his monastery, that might hold some information about the mansion."

Shaurya's eyes widened. "The monastery? That's miles away!" he exclaimed.

Parvati nodded. "But it might be the only way to find out what the blue light is, and why it's there."

A tense silence filled the room, broken only by the rhythmic chirping of crickets outside. Shaurya and Parvati exchanged a look, a silent understanding passing between them. Their childhood adventures had always been fueled by curiosity and a shared sense of fun. This time, however, the stakes were higher, the fear of the unknown more potent.

"Maybe we can ask someone to take us," Shaurya suggested, his voice betraying a hint of fear.

Parvati shook her head. "The journey is long and potentially dangerous. We can't risk involving anyone else."

Shaurya fell silent, his face etched with worry. He knew Parvati's determination was unwavering. Yet, venturing out into the unknown, far from the familiar comfort of Suhana, filled him with trepidation.

Taking a deep breath, Parvati reached out and squeezed Shaurya's hand reassuringly. "We don't have to do this alone," she said, her voice firm despite her own anxieties. "We can plan, find the right supplies, and maybe even ask Nani Amma for her advice."

Shaurya squeezed her hand back, a flicker of determination replacing his fear. "Okay," he said, his voice gaining strength. "But if it gets too spooky, we turn back, right?"

Parvati smiled, a spark of relief lighting up her face. "Deal," she agreed.

Together, they hatched a plan, a secret pact fueled by their unwavering curiosity and a tinge of apprehension. They knew the journey to the monastery wouldn't be easy, but the allure of unraveling the mysteries of the abandoned mansion and the blue light proved too strong to resist. They were determined to find answers, even if it meant venturing into the heart of the unknown.

The following days were a whirlwind of hushed conversations and meticulous planning. Parvati and Shaurya, sworn to secrecy, spent their evenings huddled beneath a sprawling mango tree at the edge of the village, away from prying eyes and gossiping ears.

Parvati consulted Nani Amma, seeking not just her knowledge but also her blessing for their clandestine journey. Nani Amma, though surprised by their desire to delve into the secrets of the mansion, listened patiently. She recounted stories passed down through generations, tales of the mansion's enigmatic past and the whispers of a powerful artifact rumored to be hidden within its walls.

"The stories warn of a dormant power," Nani Amma said, her voice laced with a hint of caution, "a force that could be awoken by those with the wrong intentions."

Parvati and Shaurya exchanged nervous glances. The blue light, the whispers of a curse, and now a dormant power - the mansion seemed to hold more secrets than they had bargained for. However, their resolve remained unshaken.

Nani Amma, sensing their unwavering determination, relented. She offered them a simple map leading to the monastery, a well-worn piece of parchment marked with faded trails and cryptic symbols. She also provided them with sturdy knapsacks filled with dried fruits, roasted nuts, and a small pouch of coins for any unexpected needs during their journey.

The night before their departure, a cloak of nervous excitement hung heavy in the air.

Parvati, unable to sleep, tossed and turned in her cot. Visions of the desolate mansion, the flickering blue light, and the unknown dangers that lay ahead danced behind her closed eyelids.

Shaurya, similarly restless, snuck out of his room and joined Parvati under the mango tree. They sat in comfortable silence, the moon casting a silvery glow on their faces, a silent promise hanging between them.

As the first rays of dawn painted the sky, Parvati and Shaurya stole out of the village, their knapsacks slung over their shoulders and hearts pounding with a mix of excitement and apprehension. They were well aware that their journey wouldn't be a simple walk through the countryside. The path to the monastery, according to Nani Amma's map, wound through dense forests and across treacherous mountain passes. But they were determined, fueled by an insatiable curiosity and a shared sense of adventure.

The first leg of their journey led them through familiar plains, dotted with fields of swaying green. The air was filled with the chirping of birds and the gentle hum of insects. Yet, a sense of unease gnawed at their insides. With every step further from the village, the comfort of home receded, replaced by the vast unknown that stretched before them.

As the day wore on, the landscape transformed. Lush green fields gave way to dense forests, the sunlight struggling to penetrate the thick canopy of leaves. The chirping of birds was replaced by the eerie calls of unseen creatures. The air grew heavy with humidity, and the path narrowed, winding through a maze of gnarled trees and thorny undergrowth.

Fatigue began to set in, and a sense of doubt crept into their minds. Had they bitten off more than they could chew? Was their quest for answers worth venturing so far from the familiar comfort of their village?

Just as despair threatened to consume them, they stumbled upon a clearing. A small, gurgling stream snaked its way through the heart of the clearing, its crystal-clear water reflecting the dappled sunlight filtering through the leaves. Relief washed over them, and they collapsed onto the grassy bank, fatigue momentarily forgotten.

As they quenched their thirst from the cool stream, a sense of calmness descended upon them. The whisper of the stream and the gentle rustling of leaves seemed to offer a sense of solace, a reassurance that they weren't entirely alone in this vast wilderness.

Rejuvenated by the brief respite, Parvati and Shaurya decided to make camp for the night. Gathering dry twigs and leaves, they managed to build a small fire, its flickering flames offering them warmth and a sense of security. As the stars emerged, painting the night sky with a dazzling display, they huddled closer, sharing stories and dreams, their fear momentarily replaced by a sense of camaraderie.

The first night under the open sky was a stark contrast to the comfort of their beds in Suhana. The unfamiliar sounds of the forest, the rustling of leaves in the wind, and the distant hooting of owls kept them on edge. However, Parvati and Shaurya found solace in each other's presence. They were in this adventure together, and together they would face whatever challenges lay ahead.

As the night deepened, the fire crackled merrily, casting flickering shadows that danced on the surrounding trees. Parvati gazed into the flames, her mind swirling with a mix of excitement and apprehension.

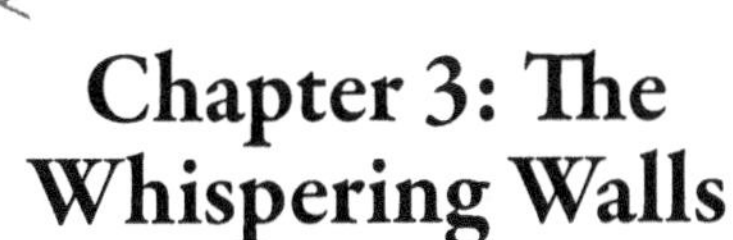

Chapter 3: The Whispering Walls

The days that followed blurred into a continuous trek through the dense wilderness. Parvati and Shaurya followed Nani Amma's map, their progress slow and arduous. The dense forest canopy blocked most of the sunlight, creating a perpetual twilight beneath the emerald tapestry of leaves. The air hung heavy with the scent of damp earth and decaying leaves, punctuated by the occasional chirp of an unseen bird or the rustling of unseen creatures in the undergrowth.

Despite their youthful resilience, fatigue began to gnaw at them. Hunger pangs became a constant companion, their meager supplies dwindling faster than anticipated. The initial excitement of the adventure had given way to a gnawing sense of doubt. Were they truly on the right path? Had they underestimated the dangers of the forest?

One particularly grueling afternoon, as they stumbled through a maze of tangled vines and thorny bushes, despair threatened to overwhelm them. Just as they were about to give up, a sliver of sunlight pierced through the dense foliage, illuminating a narrow path ahead. With renewed hope, they pushed forward, the path leading them to a small clearing.

In the center of the clearing stood a weathered stone structure, partially concealed by creeping vines and moss. It wasn't the magnificent monastery they had envisioned, but it offered a welcome respite from the relentless forest. As they approached, the inscription above the arched doorway became legible - a forgotten language that defied their understanding.

Hope surged through them. Could this be a sign? Perhaps this ancient structure held clues that could lead them to the monastery, or even offer some insight into the secrets of the abandoned mansion.

Cautiously, they pushed open the creaking wooden doors, revealing a dark and dusty interior. A stale, musty smell assaulted their nostrils as they stepped inside. The air was thick with an oppressive silence, broken only by the faint drip of water from somewhere in the distance.

Squinting through the dimness, their eyes adjusted to the gloom. The room they stood in appeared to be a deserted temple, its walls adorned with faded murals depicting scenes of a bygone era. Strange symbols and figures, seemingly dancing in a forgotten ritual, stared back at them.

Parvati shivered, a sense of unease prickling her skin. The air in the room felt thick with an unseen energy, a tangible reminder of the passage of time and the forgotten secrets it held.

Taking a deep breath, they ventured further into the structure. The room led to a series of narrow corridors, each one darker and more oppressive than the last. Cobwebs brushed against their faces, and the stench of dampness grew stronger. The silence was punctuated only by the echo of their own footsteps, an unsettling reminder of their isolation.

As they navigated the labyrinthine corridors, they stumbled upon a chamber unlike any other. The room, slightly larger than the others, housed a weathered wooden table and a single, flickering oil lamp that cast long, dancing shadows on the walls. On the table lay a collection of dusty scrolls and leather-bound books, their pages filled with strange symbols and cryptic writing.

Excitement bubbled within them. Could this be the repository of ancient knowledge Panditji spoke of? Could these scrolls hold the key to unlocking the mysteries of the mansion?

Their hearts pounded with anticipation as they cautiously approached the table. Parvati reached out and gingerly lifted one of the leather-bound books. The worn cover felt cool and dry beneath her fingertips. She opened it, revealing pages filled with intricate symbols and faded script. The language was unfamiliar, yet it emanated an aura of power and forgotten knowledge.

Shaurya, equally curious, reached for a scroll tied with a faded ribbon. As he unfurled it, a soft rustling sound filled the chamber. A draft of air, seemingly out of nowhere, swept through the room, extinguishing the flickering oil lamp and plunging them into darkness.

Panic surged through them. Trapped in a tomb-like chamber, surrounded by cryptic symbols and the whispers of the past, their initial excitement morphed into a chilling fear.

Blindness descended upon them, the oppressive darkness amplifying the silence to an almost unbearable degree. Shaurya fumbled in his knapsack, his fingers searching for the flint and tinder they had packed for emergencies. After what seemed like an eternity, a spark flared to life, illuminating a sliver of the chamber.

The flickering light danced upon the ancient murals, lending them an eerie animation. The strange symbols seemed to writhe and twist, their enigmatic forms taking on a menacing life of their own. Parvati felt a cold sweat prickle her skin, a primal fear gripping her heart.

"Shaurya," she whispered, her voice barely audible in the suffocating silence. "Do you hear that?"

Shaurya strained his ears. A faint sound, almost imperceptible at first, filled the chamber. It was a low hum, a vibration that seemed to emanate from the very walls themselves. The rhythmic thrumming resonated within their bones, sending shivers down their spines.

The fear that had been simmering within them reached a boiling point. This wasn't just an abandoned structure; it held a hidden power, a malevolent force awakened by their intrusion. The whispers of the past, trapped within these walls, were beginning to stir.

With a shared look of terror, they knew they couldn't stay here any longer. The darkness, the pulsating hum, and the oppressive atmosphere were closing in on them. Clutching the leather-bound book and the scroll in their trembling hands, they stumbled back towards the corridor, their hearts pounding a frantic rhythm against their ribs.

The journey back through the maze of corridors seemed endless. The shadows danced and stretched, morphing into monstrous shapes in the flickering light of Shaurya's makeshift torch. Every creak of the ancient structure, every rustle of unseen creatures, amplified their fear.

Finally, they burst back into the clearing, the sight of the open sky a beacon of hope. They didn't waste time exploring the rest of the structure. Their sole focus was on getting out of there, as far away from the unsettling hum and cryptic symbols as possible.

Emerging from the dense forest, they stumbled back onto the path leading towards the monastery. They walked through the night, fueled by adrenaline and a desperate urge to put as much distance between them and the ancient structure as possible.

The first rays of dawn painted the sky a fiery orange as they finally collapsed in exhaustion under a giant banyan tree. The events of the past night replayed in their minds, a chilling reminder of the power they had inadvertently awakened.

Parvati opened the leather-bound book, her eyes scanning the unfamiliar symbols. Perhaps, within these pages, lay an explanation for the unsettling hum and the malevolent energy they had felt in the chamber. But would she dare to decipher its secrets?

Shaurya unfurled the scroll, the cryptic symbols etched upon its surface defying comprehension. Was the knowledge they sought hidden within these ancient markings? And if they did manage to unlock its secrets, would it be a blessing or a curse?

One thing was clear: their quest for answers had taken an unexpected and terrifying turn. The secrets of the abandoned mansion seemed to be intertwined with a far more ancient and powerful force, a force they had unwittingly disturbed. The journey ahead, they realized with a growing sense of dread, would be far more perilous than they had ever imagined.

Old Man Ravi's unexpected appearance sent a jolt through Parvati and Shaurya. Relief battled with apprehension. Here was a familiar face, but would he believe their fantastical story about the abandoned structure, the pulsating hum, and the ancient scrolls?

Stammering slightly, Parvati blurted out a fabricated explanation. They were lost, she said, venturing deeper into the forest than they intended while searching for medicinal herbs. Shame burned in her cheeks, but the thought of revealing their true purpose and the unsettling secrets they had stumbled upon was too terrifying.

Old Man Ravi studied them with a piercing gaze, his rheumy eyes seeming to see right through their flimsy lie. A knowing smile played on his lips, a hint of amusement crinkling the corners of his eyes.

"Lost, are we?" he rasped, his voice dry as fallen leaves. "The forest can be a tricky place, especially for those who stray from the beaten path."

Parvati and Shaurya exchanged a wary glance. Old Man Ravi's cryptic words sent shivers down their spines. Did he know more than he was letting on?

"We were hoping you could point us in the right direction," Shaurya said, forcing a smile.

Old Man Ravi stroked his long, wiry beard thoughtfully. "The way back to Suhana is long and treacherous," he said, his voice low and rumbling. "But I might be able to help you, on one condition."

Parvati's heart pounded in her chest. A condition? What did he want in exchange for his help?

"What condition?" she blurted out before she could stop herself.

Old Man Ravi's smile widened. "Tell me, children," he said, his voice laced with a hint of curiosity, "what brings you so deep into the wilderness?"

Parvati hesitated, her mind racing. Could they trust him? A part of her yearned to confide in him, to share the burden of their secret. But another part, the voice of caution, held her back.

Sensing their apprehension, Old Man Ravi chuckled, a dry rasping sound that echoed through the trees. "Don't worry, children," he said. "Your secrets are safe with me. I have no interest in the gossip of villagers."

His words held a surprising sincerity, and a flicker of hope ignited within Parvati. Perhaps, just perhaps, they had found an unlikely ally.

Taking a deep breath, she decided to take a chance. In a hushed voice, she recounted their encounter with Panditji, the whispers about the abandoned mansion, and their discovery of the ancient structure. She left out the details about the blue light, fearing it would raise further questions.

As she spoke, Old Man Ravi listened intently, his expression unreadable. When she finished, a long silence hung heavy in the air, broken only by the chirping of unseen birds.

Finally, Old Man Ravi spoke, his voice low and gravelly. "The place you describe," he said, "is known by some as the Whispering Walls. It is an ancient structure, shrouded in time and whispered legends."

A shiver ran down Parvati's spine. Whispering Walls. The name sent a jolt of recognition. Nani Amma had mentioned a place by that very name, a place rumored to hold forgotten knowledge and secrets best left undisturbed.

"Do you know anything about the symbols in the book and scroll we found?" Shaurya blurted out, his curiosity overcoming his apprehension.

Old Man Ravi's eyes narrowed. "The language of those symbols," he said, his voice barely a whisper, "is older than time itself. It is the language of a forgotten civilization, a language that speaks of power and knowledge beyond mortal comprehension."

Parvati's breath hitched. The book and scroll held the key to a forgotten civilization? The weight of their discovery settled upon her like a heavy cloak.

"And the pulsating hum?" Shaurya asked, his voice barely audible. "What did it mean?"

Old Man Ravi's gaze drifted towards the distant mountains, his face etched with a solemn expression. "The hum," he said, his voice low and grave, "is an awakening. It is a sign that the secrets held within the Whispering Walls are stirring, and forces long dormant are beginning to rise."

Parvati and Shaurya exchanged a panicked glance. They had unwittingly awakened something ancient and powerful, something they were completely unprepared to face.

"But what do we do now?" Parvati whispered, her voice trembling with fear.

Old Man Ravi turned back to them, a resolute glint in his eyes. "The path ahead is fraught with danger," he said, his voice firm. "But knowledge is power, and the knowledge within those scrolls might be the only thing that can stop what you've unleashed," Old Man Ravi finished, his voice carrying a weight of responsibility.

Parvati and Shaurya felt a surge of hope battling the fear that had gripped them. Here was a path forward, a way to undo the damage they might have caused.

"But how do we decipher the scrolls?" Shaurya asked, his voice laced with urgency. "The symbols are beyond anything we've ever seen."

Old Man Ravi stroked his beard thoughtfully. "There might be someone who can help," he said, his voice low. "But this person resides far from here, deep within the hidden valley of the Oracles."

The Oracles. Parvati had heard whispers of them, mythical figures said to possess ancient knowledge and the ability to commune with the spirits of the past. Could they be the key to understanding the scrolls and unlocking the secrets of the Whispering Walls?

"The journey to the Oracles is long and perilous," Old Man Ravi warned, his gaze fixed on them. "It requires navigating treacherous mountain passes and facing dangers that can test even the bravest hearts."

Parvati and Shaurya exchanged a determined look. They had come too far to turn back now. The weight of responsibility, the knowledge that they had awakened something powerful, settled heavily upon them. They had to see this through.

"We'll do it," Parvati said, her voice firm despite the tremor in her heart. "We have to."

Old Man Ravi nodded, a flicker of approval in his eyes. "Then let me guide you as far as I can," he said. "The path to the mountains is treacherous, and your journey will be easier with someone who knows these woods."

Relief washed over Parvati and Shaurya. They weren't alone in this. Old Man Ravi, despite his unconventional ways, offered a glimmer of hope, a guide on the perilous path ahead.

The following days were a blur of activity. Under Old Man Ravi's tutelage, they learned essential survival skills: how to hunt for food, navigate by the stars, and set traps for dangers lurking in the forest. They learned about the local flora and fauna, which plants could be used for sustenance and which ones to avoid, the calls of birds that signaled danger, and the rustling of leaves that betrayed the presence of unseen predators.

Old Man Ravi also revealed his own knowledge of the Whispering Walls, though it was fragmented and laced with cryptic warnings. He spoke of a powerful artifact rumored to be hidden within the structure, an artifact capable of immense good or unimaginable destruction.

As they trekked deeper into the wilderness, the landscape shifted. Lush forests gave way to rugged mountains, their peaks scraping the clouds. The air grew colder, and the wind whistled a haunting tune through the jagged rock formations.

Finally, after days of arduous travel, they reached the foothills of the mountain range that supposedly led to the hidden valley of the Oracles. The path ahead was a daunting one – a narrow, winding trail that clung precariously to the side of a towering mountain, disappearing into a misty veil above.

"This is as far as I can go," Old Man Ravi said, his voice gruff with emotion. "The dangers beyond are far greater than anything you've faced so far."

Parvati felt a pang of sadness. Though their time together had been short, Old Man Ravi had become a trusted guide and a source of comfort on this unexpected journey.

Shaurya stepped forward and clasped Old Man Ravi's hand in a firm grip. "Thank you," he said, his voice sincere. "You've given us a chance."

Old Man Ravi returned the handshake, a flicker of pride in his eyes. "Remember," he said, his voice filled with a quiet intensity, "knowledge is power, but wisdom is the key to wielding it. Don't let fear cloud your judgment, and never underestimate the strength within yourselves."

With a final nod, Old Man Ravi turned and disappeared back into the dense forest, leaving Parvati and Shaurya standing alone at the foot of the treacherous mountain path. They took a deep breath, their eyes locked in silent understanding. The journey to the Oracles, and the secrets they held, awaited.

With hearts pounding with a mix of anticipation and apprehension, Parvati and Shaurya stepped onto the narrow trail, their eyes fixed on the misty peak that seemed to pierce the heavens. They were determined to find answers, to unravel the mysteries of the abandoned mansion and the blue light, and to face whatever dangers lay ahead. Their quest for childhood curiosity had morphed into a mission of responsibility, a burden they were now determined to carry. With each step they took on the treacherous mountain path, they knew that their lives, and the fate of their village.

Chapter 4: Whispers on the Wind

The mountain path snaked its way precariously up the face of the sheer rock face. Parvati and Shaurya, hearts hammering in their chests, carefully navigated the uneven terrain. Below them, the forest floor fell away in a dizzying descent, shrouded in a perpetual mist. The air grew thinner, each breath a struggle in the chilling altitude.

The knowledge of Old Man Ravi's warnings hung heavy in the air. Each rustle in the undergrowth, each screech of an unseen bird, sent shivers down their spines. Yet, they pressed on, driven by a newfound sense of purpose and the weight of responsibility that rested upon their young shoulders.

Days bled into nights, a blur of relentless climbing and bone-chilling nights spent huddled beneath precarious overhangs, gnawing on dried rations and shivering in the thin mountain air. They battled exhaustion, hunger, and the constant gnawing fear of a misstep that could send them plummeting to a certain death.

One particularly grueling afternoon, just as fatigue threatened to overwhelm them, they emerged from a particularly treacherous stretch of the path to find themselves at a narrow plateau. Relief washed over them as they collapsed onto the rocky ground, their bodies spent.

The plateau offered a breathtaking vista. Lush green valleys stretched out before them, dotted with sparkling streams and ringed by snow-capped peaks that pierced the azure sky. Yet, their gaze was instantly drawn to a cluster of buildings nestled amidst the verdant expanse – a hidden haven shrouded in a mystical aura.

"Could that be it?" Shaurya whispered, his voice barely audible over the howling wind.

Parvati squinted through the distance. The buildings, constructed from a smooth, white stone that seemed to shimmer in the sunlight, resembled a small monastery. Smoke curled from chimneys, hinting at life within. Could this be the fabled valley of the Oracles, their only hope to decipher the scrolls and unravel the secrets they held?

A surge of renewed energy coursed through them. They had made it to the first leg of their journey. Now, the true challenge awaited them – gaining the trust of the Oracles and convincing them to help.

With newfound determination, they descended the treacherous slope leading to the valley floor. As they approached the buildings, a sense of serenity washed over them. The air vibrated with a quiet energy, and an ethereal calmness soothed their frayed nerves.

An elderly woman, her face etched with age and wisdom, stood waiting at the entrance to the main building. Her eyes, the color of faded jade, held a warmth that belied her age.

Parvati and Shaurya exchanged a nervous glance. This was it. The moment of truth.

Taking a deep breath, Parvati stepped forward. In a voice trembling with both fear and resolve, she recounted their journey – their encounter with Panditji, the rumors surrounding the abandoned mansion, their discovery of the Whispering Walls, and their fateful meeting with Old Man Ravi.

The Oracle woman listened intently, her expression unreadable. When Parvati finished, a long silence hung heavy in the air.

"You have embarked on a perilous path, young ones," the Oracle woman finally spoke, her voice low and melodic. "The secrets you seek are not meant for the untrained eye."

Disappointment threatened to consume Parvati. Had they come all this way in vain? Would the Oracles refuse to help?

Sensing their despair, the woman offered a gentle smile. "However," she continued, "your courage and determination are commendable. The fate of your village may indeed be intertwined with the secrets you hold."

Hope flickered in Parvati's heart. "Then you will help us?" Shaurya blurted out, his voice filled with eagerness.

The Oracle woman chuckled softly. "Help you decipher the scrolls, perhaps. But true understanding comes from within, young ones. You must be willing to confront your fears and delve into the depths of your own knowledge."

Her words were cryptic, but they held a spark of hope. Over the next few weeks, Parvati and Shaurya became apprentices to the Oracles. They learned about the history of the land, the ancient civilizations that once thrived there, and the forgotten language etched within the scrolls they carried.

The Oracles, wise and patient, guided them through the labyrinthine symbols, revealing their deeper meanings and the forgotten power they held. They spoke of the potential for immense good, but also the devastating consequences that could be unleashed if the knowledge within the scrolls fell into the wrong hands.

As days turned into weeks, Parvati discovered a hidden talent for languages. The forgotten symbols, once indecipherable, began to unlock their secrets, revealing a history far older and more complex than they ever imagined. The scroll spoke of a powerful artifact, a source of immense energy hidden within the Whispering Walls.

The information gleaned from the scroll sent shivers down their spines. The artifact it described, known as the "Heart of Anya," was said to be a pulsating crystal capable of harnessing the very life force of the earth. In the right hands, it could bring prosperity and healing. However, in the wrong grasp, it could unleash a devastating torrent of energy, warping the land and corrupting the souls of those around it.

The inscription on the scroll spoke of a prophecy - a chosen one who would wield the artifact's power for the good of all. The chosen one would possess a pure heart and a deep connection to the land. Parvati and Shaurya exchanged a hesitant glance. Could one of them be the chosen one? The thought was both exhilarating and terrifying.

Meanwhile, Shaurya found himself drawn to the intricacies of the ancient murals adorning the walls of the Oracle's dwelling. These murals depicted scenes of a glorious civilization that had harnessed the power of the Heart of Anya for their benefit. It showed lush landscapes, thriving cities, and a society in harmony with nature. However, other panels depicted a darker turn of events - monstrous creatures with glowing red eyes, ravaged lands, and a society consumed by greed and violence.

The transition between the two halves of the mural was a single, haunting image - a figure, shrouded in shadow, reaching out to grasp the Heart of Anya. The inscription beneath it was a stark warning: "Beware the Shadow's grasp, for it will twist the heart and corrupt the pure."

These revelations filled Parvati and Shaurya with a chilling sense of urgency. They understood the dangers lurking within the Whispering Walls and the devastating consequences if the artifact fell into the wrong hands. The question remained – who was the Shadow?

The Oracle woman noticed their growing unease. One evening, under a canopy of starlit sky, she summoned them for a private conversation.

"You have learned much, young ones," she said, her voice soft yet filled with a quiet strength. "But knowledge alone is not enough. You must also be prepared for the challenges that lie ahead."

She then revealed a chilling truth. An ancient order, known as the Shadows of Anya, had long coveted the artifact's power. They believed it held the key to achieving immortality and ultimate dominion over the world. For centuries, they had searched for the Heart of Anya, and now, with the awakening of the Whispering Walls, they would likely be drawn to its location.

Parvati felt a cold dread grip her heart. The Shadows of Anya – they were the embodiment of the warning etched on the mural. Their path was leading them straight into the heart of a dangerous game, a battle for the fate of the world, a battle they were woefully unprepared for.

"How do we fight them?" Shaurya blurted out, his voice laced with fear and defiance.

The Oracle woman smiled sadly. "The scrolls and murals hold the key, young ones," she said.

"They speak of trials to be overcome and a test of your true strength. You must train, hone your skills, and delve deeper into the wisdom of your ancestors. Only then will you be ready to face the Shadows and protect the Heart of Anya."

The following months were a grueling test of both body and spirit. The Oracles put Parvati and Shaurya through a rigorous training regime. They learned hand-to-hand combat, the art of stealth and deception, and the use of ancient herbal remedies. They practiced meditation, seeking to tap into their inner strength and connect with the spiritual energy that flowed through the land.

Parvati, fueled by a burgeoning sense of responsibility, trained relentlessly. She discovered a hidden agility and a surprising strength within herself. She learned to channel her fear into focus, her anxiety into determination. Under the tutelage of the Oracles, she honed her understanding of the ancient language, delving deeper into the cryptic messages embedded within the scrolls.

Shaurya, on the other hand, found his calling in deciphering the ancient murals. He spent countless hours studying every detail, uncovering hidden patterns and symbols. With each passing day, he developed a growing connection to the forgotten civilization, their triumphs and their ultimate downfall. He learned to translate their warnings into strategies, their mistakes into lessons for the battles to come.

As the weeks morphed into months, a bond of deep friendship and unwavering trust blossomed between Parvati and Shaurya. They relied on each other for support, encouragement, and a shared sense of purpose. They were no longer just childhood friends; they were warriors in training, united by a common cause.

Finally, after months of intense preparation, the Oracle woman announced that the time for their return had come. Though apprehensive about the dangers that awaited them, Parvati and Shaurya were also filled with a sense of resolute determination. They had a plan, albeit a loose one. The information gleaned from the scrolls and murals offered a fragmented roadmap. The inscription hinted at a series of trials guarding the Heart of Anya, trials designed to test the chosen one's strength, courage, and purity of heart.

Armed with this knowledge and their newfound skills, Parvati and Shaurya bid farewell to the Oracles, their hearts heavy with gratitude and a touch of fear. The serenity of the hidden valley felt distant now, replaced by the looming dangers beyond the mountain pass.

Their descent was quicker, fueled by a renewed purpose. Yet, the treacherous path remained a constant reminder of the challenges ahead. As they emerged from the foothills and set foot on familiar ground, a wave of nostalgia washed over them. But their once carefree village now seemed shrouded in a thin veil of worry.

Their return caused a stir. Whispers flew like startled birds as villagers gathered around them, eager to hear of their adventures. Parvati and Shaurya, however, were focused on their mission. They sought Panditji, the village elder, hoping to glean any information he might have about the Whispering Walls or the trials they might face.

Panditji, upon hearing their tale, looked older than his years. His eyes, usually filled with a twinkle of amusement, were now clouded with worry. He confirmed their suspicions – whispers of the Shadows of Anya had reached the village long ago, though their reach had, until now, remained limited to hushed warnings and campfire stories.

Unfortunately, Panditji didn't have any concrete information about the trials or the location of the Whispering Walls. However, he offered a cryptic clue. "The entrance," he mumbled, tracing a circle in the dirt with his gnarled finger, "lies hidden where the wind whispers secrets to the ancient stones."

This cryptic message provided little comfort, but it was a starting point. Parvati and Shaurya, armed with their knowledge and their newfound abilities, decided to start their search at the abandoned temple where they had first encountered Panditji.

The once familiar surroundings appeared different now. The crumbling structure seemed to hold a hidden energy, as if the whispers of the past had grown louder. As they explored the dusty chambers, a sudden gust of wind swirled around them, sending shivers down their spines.

The wind seemed to carry a faint melody, a haunting tune that tugged at their memories. Shaurya, his eyes gleaming with recognition, pointed towards a hidden niche in the wall. It had been concealed by cobwebs, but the wind had momentarily cleared the obstruction.

Within the niche, a faint inscription shimmered in the dim light. It was written in the same language as the scroll, a language they now understood. With bated breath, Parvati deciphered the inscription: "Speak the forgotten words, and the gateway shall open."

Their hearts pounded with a mixture of excitement and trepidation. Could this be the entrance Panditji spoke of? Parvati recalled a phrase from the scroll, a verse that spoke of a connection between the wind and the ancient stones. Taking a deep breath, she chanted the verse, her voice echoing through the chamber.

The walls trembled. A low groan reverberated through the structure, and dust rained down in a cascade. A hidden section of the wall slid open, revealing a dark passage leading downwards. This was it. The entrance to the Whispering Walls.

Parvati and Shaurya exchanged a nervous glance. The journey they had embarked on, a childhood curiosity that spiraled into a perilous quest, was about to take its next terrifying step. With a deep breath and a shared look of determination, they stepped into the darkness, the chilling whisper of the wind urging them forward.

The passage plunged them into an inky blackness. The air grew heavy and damp, carrying the faint scent of mildew and something far older, something elemental and untamed. Their only source of light was the flickering glow of a small clay lamp Shaurya had managed to salvage from the abandoned temple.

The passage sloped downwards, its surface slick with moisture. They navigated the uneven path carefully, their senses heightened, listening for any sound that might indicate danger. The silence was broken only by the rhythmic drip of water somewhere deeper within the stone belly of the mountain.

After what felt like an eternity, the passage opened into a vast cavern. The air hung thick with a strange luminescence, emanating from glowing fungi clinging to the cavern walls. The sight was both awe-inspiring and unnerving. Towering stalactites dripped precariously from the ceiling, casting long, ominous shadows across the cavern floor.

As their eyes adjusted to the dim light, they noticed a series of stone pillars arranged in a circular pattern at the center of the cavern. Etchings adorned the pillars, depicting creatures they had only seen in the ancient murals - monstrous figures with glowing red eyes and twisted bodies. These were the servants of the Shadows of Anya, grotesque guardians of the secrets hidden within.

A sudden tremor shook the cavern floor, sending a shower of dust cascading down from the stalactites. Fear prickled at Parvati's skin. Was this the first test? Were they already under attack?

Shaurya, ever the strategist, observed the pillars and noticed faint symbols etched on their base. These were variations of the symbols they had studied in the scrolls. "The inscription," he whispered, pointing towards a central platform adorned with a similar symbol.

Parvati recalled the scroll's description of the first trial – a test of knowledge. It spoke of an ancient riddle, the answer to which would open a passage leading deeper into the Whispering Walls. Stepping closer to the platform, she traced the intricate symbol with her finger, murmuring a prayer for guidance.

A voice boomed from within the cavern, resonating throughout the chamber. It was a voice devoid of humanity, a chilling rasp that sent shivers down their spines.

"Seekers of forbidden knowledge," the voice echoed, "answer the riddle and prove your worth.

Failure will result in your demise!"

Parvati took a deep breath, trying to quiet the tremor in her voice. Recalling the knowledge gleaned from the Oracles, she focused on the inscription. It resembled a stylized eye, a symbol of wisdom in the ancient language.

Suddenly, a memory surfaced from her childhood – a riddle her grandfather used to tell them under the starlit sky. It spoke of a silent witness that saw everything but spoke nothing. The answer, etched in her mind, was clear.

Taking a deep breath, Parvati turned towards the echoing voice. "The answer," she declared, her voice ringing with newfound confidence, "is the moon!"

The cavern vibrated with a low hum. Then, with a deafening roar, a section of the wall behind the central platform groaned open, revealing another passage shrouded in darkness. The first trial had been passed.

Relief washed over them, tinged with a touch of apprehension. They had faced their first challenge, but there were surely many more to come. They exchanged a determined look, a wordless promise to stand by each other. With newfound courage, they stepped into the darkness, the echoing voice of the cavern a chilling reminder that they were not alone.

The passage leading deeper into the Whispering Walls was a labyrinth of twisting tunnels and dark chambers. They faced a series of trials designed to test their skills – tests of strength, agility, and mental fortitude. Each challenge drew upon the knowledge gleaned from the scrolls and the training received from the Oracles.

In one chamber, they dodged razor-sharp blades propelled by hidden traps. In another, they navigated a maze of illusions, relying on their wits and sense of touch to find the way out. Each challenge brought them closer to the Heart of Anya, pushing them to the limits of their abilities.

As they progressed, the whispers on the wind grew louder, no longer a faint hum but a cacophony of voices – voices of the past, guardians of the secrets, and perhaps even the shadows themselves. These whispers spoke of forgotten lore, of the dangers that awaited them, and of the power that resided at the heart of the Whispering Walls.

Through it all, Parvati and Shaurya remained steadfast. They drew strength from their shared purpose, from the bond forged in the hidden valley of the Oracles. They learned to tap into a deeper well of courage within themselves, a wellspring of power stronger than they had ever imagined.

Finally, after days of relentless trials, they emerged into a vast cavern unlike any they had seen before. The cavern pulsed with an ethereal

Chapter 5: Echoes in the Stone

The vast cavern pulsed with an ethereal light, emanating from a central crystal that shimmered with an otherworldly glow. It was the Heart of Anya, the source of immense power that they had been relentlessly pursuing. The air crackled with raw energy, sending a jolt through Parvati and Shaurya. They had reached the heart of the Whispering Walls, the culmination of their perilous journey.

But their elation was short-lived. A menacing figure stood guard before the crystal, a dark silhouette against the pulsating light. It was tall and cloaked in shadowy robes, its face obscured by a hood. An aura of malevolent power radiated from it, chilling Parvati and Shaurya to the bone.

"So," the figure rasped, its voice a guttural whisper that echoed through the cavern, "you have finally reached the Heart of Anya. But are you worthy of its power?"

Parvati recognized the figure instantly. It was a Shadow of Anya, the embodiment of the dark prophecy they had learned about in the valley. Fear threatened to paralyze her, but years of training and a deep-seated desire to protect her village fueled her courage.

"We are not here for your power," she declared, her voice surprisingly steady. "We are here to ensure it doesn't fall into the wrong hands."

The Shadow let out a chilling chuckle. "Foolish children," it rasped. "You have no idea of the power you seek to control. In the wrong hands, it could bring peace. In the right hands, it could create an empire."

Its words were laced with a seductive power, a warped promise of a world reshaped to its will. Parvati could almost feel the allure of the limitless potential, the intoxicating rush of power at her fingertips. But she quickly pushed aside the temptation.

"The prophecy speaks of a chosen one," she countered, her voice unwavering. "Someone pure of heart who will use its power for good."

The figure tilted its head, a flicker of amusement dancing in the darkness beneath its hood.

"Prophecies are easily misinterpreted," it sneered. "Perhaps you misunderstand your role in this game."

A tense silence descended upon the cavern. The air crackled with unspoken threats, the weight of the situation hanging heavy in the air. Parvati knew a peaceful resolution was unlikely. This was a battle for the fate of the Heart of Anya, a battle that could not be avoided.

Suddenly, the Shadow raised its hand, and the cavern floor began to tremble. Shadowy tendrils pulsed into existence, snaking towards Parvati and Shaurya. They leaped back just in time, dodging the grasping tendrils that lashed out with unnatural speed.

"Foolish mortals!" the Shadow boomed, its voice echoing with power. "You dare challenge me? Prepare to face the consequences!"

The cavern erupted into chaos. The pulsating energy of the Heart of Anya intensified, fueling the Shadow's power. Shadowy creatures materialized from the darkness, grotesque parodies of the creatures depicted in the ancient murals.

With a battle cry, Parvati and Shaurya unleashed the skills they had honed for months. Parvati, drawing upon the wisdom of the ancient language, channeled her energy into a defensive barrier, deflecting the Shadow's attacks. Shaurya, his movements honed to a lethal precision, weaved through the battlefield, his strikes aimed at the Shadow's ethereal minions.

The battle raged on, a whirlwind of darkness and light, desperation and courage. Parvati, despite her newfound strength, felt overwhelmed by the sheer number of adversaries. The Shadow, fueled by the Heart of Anya's power, seemed to be everywhere at once, its attacks relentless and impossible to predict.

Just as exhaustion threatened to consume them, Shaurya landed a critical blow, disintegrating one of the shadowy creatures. He whirled towards Parvati, his voice strained but determined.

"We have to find a way to sever its connection to the Heart," he yelled, pointing towards the pulsating crystal at the center of the cavern.

Parvati nodded, understanding the importance of his words. The Shadow's power stemmed from the Heart of Anya. Severing that connection could be their only chance of victory. But how? The scrolls offered no clear guidance for such a feat.

Suddenly, a memory from their training surfaced in Parvati's mind. The Oracle woman had spoken of a "harmony of opposites," a balance that could disrupt the flow of unnatural energy. Looking around the cavern, Parvati noticed a cluster of glowing mushrooms clinging to the wall, their bioluminescent light the only source of natural illumination within the caverns.

"The light!" she shouted, a spark of hope igniting in her eyes. "We can use the natural light to counter the Shadow's energy and weaken its connection to the Heart!"

Without hesitation, Shaurya understood. He grabbed a handful of the glowing mushrooms, their light pulsating warmly in his hand. With a coordinated leap, they launched themselves towards the central crystal. The Shadow, sensing their plan, unleashed a torrent of shadowy tendrils, aiming to intercept them.

Parvati unleashed a burst of energy, creating a temporary shield that deflected the tendrils just long enough for them to reach the platform surrounding the Heart. Here, the air crackled with raw power, making their movements sluggish and their focus difficult to maintain.

Shaurya, teeth gritted in concentration, smashed the glowing mushrooms against the crystal. A wave of pure light erupted, momentarily blinding them and forcing the Shadow to recoil. The connection seemed to falter for a brief moment, the cavern plunging into a momentary darkness before the ethereal glow of the crystal returned, albeit dimmed and flickering.

The Shadow shrieked in fury, the cavern walls echoing with its rage. Its ethereal form seemed to waver momentarily, weakened by the disruption. Yet, it was far from defeated.

"Fools!" it roared, its voice a cacophony of hate.

"You cannot defy the inevitable! The Heart of Anya will be mine!"

Renewed determination filled Parvati. They had tasted victory, however fleeting. Now, they knew their strategy held some merit. They just needed a way to increase the intensity of the natural light, to further weaken the Shadow and sever its connection to the Heart.

But their options were limited. The only source of natural light was the small cluster of glowing mushrooms they had used previously. Looking around desperately, Parvati's eyes landed on the inscription etched on the platform surrounding the crystal. It depicted a complex design, a series of interconnected symbols that vaguely resembled the glowing mushrooms they had just used.

A spark of inspiration ignited in her mind. The inscription could be the key! It might hold the instructions on how to amplify the natural light, to create a beacon powerful enough to sever the Shadow's hold.

"Shaurya," she called out, her voice barely audible over the din of the battle. "Distract the Shadow! I need time to decipher the inscription."

Shaurya understood. With a battle cry, he launched himself towards the Shadow, engaging in a desperate dance of sword and shadow. Their blades clashed, sparks flying in the dim light. Though Shaurya was outmatched in terms of raw power, his agility and skills kept the Shadow momentarily occupied, giving Parvati a narrow window of opportunity.

Taking a deep breath, she knelt before the inscription. The cavern vibrated with the Shadow's attacks, making it difficult to focus. Yet, Parvati pushed on, tracing the symbols with her fingers, her knowledge of the ancient language flooding back.

The inscription spoke of a "harmony of light," a sequence of activating specific nodes within the design to create a cascading effect, amplifying the natural light to its full potential. It was a complex ritual, requiring precise timing and unwavering focus.

Parvati closed her eyes, drowning out the chaos around her. She visualized the inscription, picturing the flow of energy within the design. With a deep breath, she channeled her own energy, a spark of light emanating from her fingertips.

She touched the first node, murmuring a phrase from the inscription. A faint light pulsed from that point, connecting to the platform and bathing the cavern in a slightly more intense natural glow. The Shadow let out a shriek, its form flickering momentarily as the connection to the Heart weakened further.

Parvati continued, her movements swift and precise. Each node she activated brought forth a surge of natural light, pushing back the darkness and weakening the Shadow's hold. With each activation, the inscription glowed brighter, resonating with the power she channeled.

Suddenly, just as she was about to activate the final node, a tendril of shadow lashed out, wrapping around her arm and squeezing with bone-crushing force. Pain lanced through her, momentarily breaking her concentration. The activation sequence faltered, and the light flickered, threatening to extinguish.

"Pathetic mortal!" the Shadow roared, its voice dripping with malice. "You cannot defy the darkness!"

Just as despair threatened to consume her, a figure blurred past her. Shaurya, his face etched with determination, had landed a critical blow on the Shadow, severing the tendril and freeing Parvati from its grasp.

Undeterred by the pain, Parvati focused her remaining energy. Ignoring the throbbing in her arm, she channeled her willpower, pushing the light within the inscription to its absolute limit.

With a final surge of power, she activated the last node. The inscription blazed with an intense light, blinding white and pure. A wave of energy erupted from the platform, washing over the cavern and engulfing the Shadow in its brilliance.

THE SHADOW SHRIEKED, a sound of pure agony and rage. Its form flickered violently, the ethereal tendrils that lashed out at Parvati and Shaurya moments ago dissolving into wisps of smoke. The connection to the Heart of Anya was severed.

The cavern plunged into momentary darkness. Then, with a soft hum, the natural light from the amplified mushrooms surged, bathing the chamber in a warm, golden glow. The pulsating energy emanating from the Heart of Anya had dimmed, no longer a blinding beacon of raw power.

Parvati and Shaurya collapsed onto the platform, panting from exhaustion. Their hearts hammered in their chests, and their bodies ached with the aftereffects of the battle. But there was no time to rest. They had won the first battle, but the war was far from over.

Slowly, they crept closer to the Heart of Anya. The crystal, once pulsing with an otherworldly glow, now emanated a soft, ethereal light. It felt warm to the touch, a comforting hum resonating within their core.

As Parvati reached out to touch the crystal, a soft voice echoed through the cavern, a voice filled with ancient wisdom and boundless power.

"You have faced the darkness and emerged victorious, young ones," the voice resonated.

"Your courage and determination have served you well."

Parvati and Shaurya looked around in awe, searching for the source of the voice. But the cavern remained empty, save for the pulsating Heart of Anya.

"Who are you?" Shaurya asked, his voice filled with trepidation and respect.

"I am the guardian of the Heart," the voice replied. "I am the power it holds, the wisdom it has accumulated over millennia."

Parvati felt a surge of understanding. The Heart of Anya wasn't just a source of power; it was a repository of ancient knowledge, a conscious entity that safeguarded its secrets.

"The prophecy spoke of a chosen one," Parvati ventured, her voice barely a whisper.

"The prophecy," the voice echoed, "speaks of a balance, a harmony between light and dark. It speaks of those who can wield power not with selfish ambition, but with compassion and wisdom."

A wave of relief washed over Parvati. They hadn't misunderstood the prophecy. It wasn't about wielding raw power; it was about wielding it responsibly, for the greater good.

"What now?" Shaurya inquired, voicing the question hanging heavy in the air.

"The future remains unwritten, young ones," the voice of the Heart responded. "The choice of how to use the knowledge contained within me lies with you. But remember, power without wisdom is a dangerous weapon. Use it wisely, for the fate of your village and the world beyond rests upon your shoulders."

The message hung heavy in the air, a weight of responsibility settling upon their young hearts. They understood the gravity of their situation.

They had prevented the Heart from falling into the wrong hands, but their journey was far from over. They had to learn to wield its knowledge and power responsibly, ensuring it was used to protect and heal, not to dominate and conquer.

Gazing at the Heart of Anya, a soft glow emanating from its core, Parvati and Shaurya knew their task had just begun. They had to return to their village, share their experiences, and guide their people towards a future where the power of the Heart could be used for the betterment of all.

The journey back would be long and arduous. They had to find a way to share their encounter with the villagers, to explain the dangers they had faced and the responsibility they now carried. But they were no longer scared children. They were warriors, forged in the fires of battle, guardians of a powerful legacy.

With newfound purpose and a shared burden of responsibility, Parvati and Shaurya stepped out of the cavern, the echoes of the battle and the voice of the Heart of Anya resonating within them, guiding their steps towards an uncertain but hopeful future.

The arduous trek back to their village felt different this time. The whispering wind, once a source of unease, now carried a melody of triumph. The familiar landmarks, once mundane, held new significance – whispers of the past adventure etched into the very landscape.

Their return was met with a mixture of joy and disbelief. Villagers who had last seen them as scared children now looked upon them with awe. Tales of their bravery, whispered through the grapevine, had preceded them.

Parvati and Shaurya knew they couldn't keep the secret of the Heart of Anya hidden for long.

Gathering the villagers in the central square, they recounted their adventures – their encounter with the Oracles, the trials within the Whispering Walls, and their final confrontation with the Shadow.

Initially, met with gasps and wide-eyed wonder, the villagers slowly grew apprehensive. The danger they had faced, the power they now held dominion over, filled their hearts with a sense of trepidation.

"How can we be sure you won't misuse this power?" an elder named Prakash, known for his measured voice and cautious nature, finally voiced the collective concern.

Parvati and Shaurya understood their fear. Power, especially power of such magnitude, often corrupted. They shared the message of the Heart of Anya, the responsibility that came with its knowledge, and the importance of using it for the good of all.

They didn't have any concrete plans, but they knew they couldn't guard the Heart alone. They proposed forming a council, a group of trusted villagers who would help them navigate this new reality. The council would consist of elders like Prakash, known for their wisdom, as well as younger, energetic villagers like Anjali, a skilled herbalist, and Ravi, a quick-witted inventor.

The decision was not taken lightly. Some villagers remained wary, fearing the corrupting influence of the Heart. But ultimately, the majority saw the potential for good, the power to heal their ailing crops, to fortify their crumbling dwellings, to perhaps even cure the illness plaguing some villagers.

With the council formed, Parvati and Shaurya began their task of learning to harness the knowledge and power of the Heart of Anya. It was a slow and arduous process. The ancient script etched on the Heart itself, a language older than anything they had encountered, proved challenging to decipher.

Days turned into weeks, weeks into months. Their training revolved around meditation and concentration, seeking to tap into the energy field that emanated from the Heart. It was a delicate dance, a constant struggle to maintain balance and avoid being overwhelmed by the sheer power at their fingertips.

Meanwhile, the council focused on ways to use the Heart's power for the betterment of the village. Anjali, with her knowledge of herbs and the village's ailments, sought to unlock the Heart's healing potential. Ravi, with his inventive mind, tinkered with devices that could channel the Heart's energy for practical applications, such as improving irrigation and strengthening building materials.

Slowly, progress was made. Anjali discovered a rare herb whose medicinal properties were amplified tenfold when exposed to the Heart's energy. The concoction, administered to the sick villagers, produced remarkable results, bringing relief and hope to the ailing community.

Ravi, drawing inspiration from the ancient script, designed a rudimentary irrigation system powered by the Heart's energy. The fields, once parched and struggling, flourished under the gentle flow of revitalized water.

News of the village's newfound prosperity, brought about by the power of the Heart of Anya, spread like wildfire. From neighboring villages, delegations arrived, seeking guidance and a potential share in the Heart's blessings.

Parvati and Shaurya, now seasoned leaders, knew they faced a new challenge – navigating the politics of power sharing and ensuring the Heart's knowledge didn't fall into the wrong hands. They had to be judicious, ensuring that only those with pure intentions could access the Heart's power.

As the sun dipped below the horizon, casting long shadows across the village, Parvati and Shaurya stood gazing upon the Heart of Anya, now pulsating with a gentle, golden light. Their journey, a whirlwind of fear, courage, and the burden of responsibility, had only just begun.

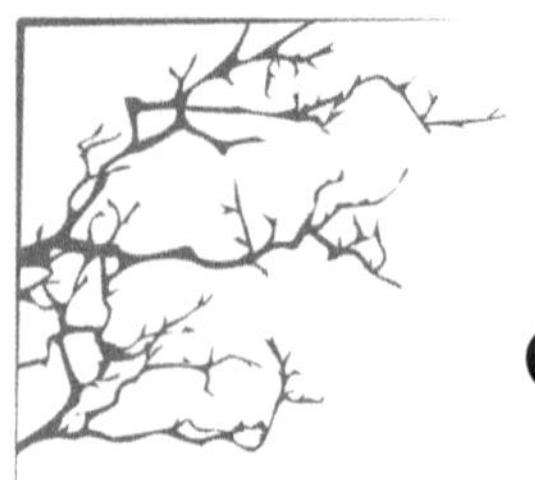

Conclusion

Years passed, and the village nestled beneath the watchful gaze of the Whispering Walls flourished. The Heart of Anya, under the stewardship of Parvati, Shaurya, and the council, became a beacon of hope, a source of knowledge and power used for the betterment of all.

The ancient script etched on the Heart yielded its secrets slowly, revealing not just spells and magical applications, but also forgotten wisdom about agriculture, healing, and sustainable living. This knowledge, shared with neighboring villages, fostered a sense of cooperation and mutual respect, a stark contrast to the previous times of suspicion and isolation.

Parvati and Shaurya, once wide-eyed children thrust into a perilous adventure, grew into wise leaders. They understood the weight of their responsibility and the delicate balance of power they held. They ensured that access to the Heart's knowledge was meritocratic, based on a commitment to the greater good.

The trials within the Whispering Walls remained a legend, a cautionary tale of the darkness that lurked in the shadows. But the villagers, empowered by their newfound knowledge and guided by the wisdom of the Heart, were no longer afraid. They knew they had the strength and the will to face any future threats.

One crisp morning, as the village bustled with activity, a group of young children, their eyes wide with wonder, approached Parvati and Shaurya. They had heard stories of their adventures, whispers of bravery and the power of the Heart.

"Tell us again about the Whispering Walls," one of the children, a bright-eyed girl named Maya, pleaded. "And the shadows you fought!"

Parvati and Shaurya exchanged a knowing smile. The past, though a powerful reminder, wouldn't define them. Their journey, fraught with danger and sacrifice, had secured a brighter future for generations to come.

As the sun rose higher, casting a warm glow over the village, Parvati began to recount their tale. The whispers of the wind carried her words, not as echoes of fear, but as a testament to courage, a reminder that even the youngest heart, when guided by wisdom and compassion, could hold immense power.

The story of the Guardians of the Heart became a cherished legend, passed down through generations. It served as a beacon, a constant reminder that the greatest power lies not in brute force, but in the courage to face darkness, the wisdom to use knowledge for good, and the unwavering belief in the potential for light to always prevail.

About the Author

Mrigendra Bharti, born on June 29, 2004, in South Delhi, India, is a multifaceted individual recognized as the owner of Mrigendra Bharti Group InfoTech India Co. Pvt Ltd. Beyond his entrepreneurial endeavors, he is a distinguished music producer, director, and a budding writer.

Embarking on his professional journey at a young age, Mrigendra Bharti's visionary leadership has led to the establishment of several successful ventures, including Croma Music Series Entertainment, Sellbrochure, Fauget Innovative, and more.

What sets Mrigendra apart is his early initiation into the world of business. His foray into the unknown realms of entrepreneurship began during his 10th-grade years, where he delved into the music industry. This initial venture laid the foundation for subsequent achievements, showcasing his dedication and resilience.

Having honed his skills in music, Mrigendra Bharti not only demonstrated significant growth in his craft but also expanded his professional network. His passion extends beyond music, encompassing app and website development, as well as graphic design.

Fueled by his creative aspirations, Mrigendra established the Mrigendra Bharti Group, a company specializing in website and app development. Currently, he collaborates with a dedicated team, collectively working on ambitious projects that promise innovation and excellence.

Mrigendra's journey serves as an inspiration, particularly for today's students, highlighting the potential of youthful determination and the ability to transform innovative ideas into successful businesses. As he continues to make strides in various domains, Mrigendra Bharti remains a dynamic force, contributing vibrancy to the realms of business, music, and technology.

Read more at https://www.imwriter-mrigendra.rf.gd.